Chester
the Rooster

Helga Moser
Illustrated by Nadia Gura

Christian Light Publications
Harrisonburg, Virginia 22802

CHESTER THE ROOSTER

Christian Light Publications, Inc.

Harrisonburg, Virginia 22802

© 2012 by Christian Light Publications, Inc.

All rights reserved. Printed in China

Third Printing, 2016

Illustrations: Nadia Gura

Cover & Interior Design: Jotham Yoder

ISBN: 978-0-87813-720-6

Acknowledgements

First, to my dear husband, Melvin, for patiently encouraging me in the writing and publishing of this book, and for being my sounding board.

Next, thanks to Nadia, who made this book come alive with her awesome paintings.

And last, but certainly not least, thanks to all the talented staff at CLP who worked to sand, polish, and shine this manuscript into publication.

I am grateful to all of you.

Note to Parents

Helga Moser bases her Pleasant Valley Farm Series on actual incidents that happened on her parents' farm. As you read the stories to your children, they will learn, along with the animals, some basic lessons of life.

This book will help your child grow in character as he learns along with Chester that pride can do a lot of damage. Had Chester thought more of others and less of himself, he wouldn't have been so foolish as to tangle with that rabbit.

Like many children, Chester had a likable personality, but when he thought too highly of himself, selfish blindness marred his character. The next time the children who read this story hear a rooster crow, may they remember Chester and the lesson Molly had to teach him.

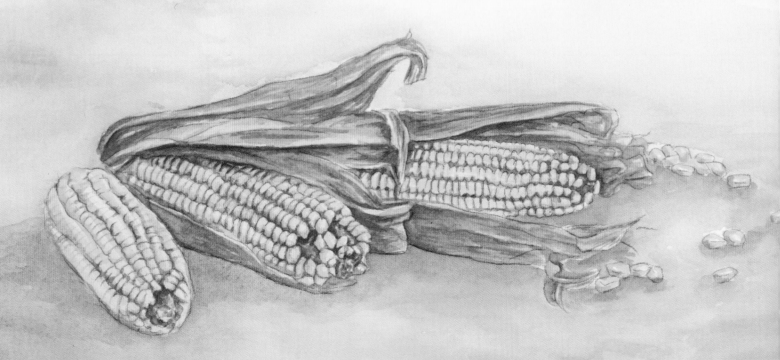

Dedication

To Justin, Thayne, Kaid, Kidron, Keaton,
Krista, and Caleb who have taught me
lessons in pride and humility.
May each of you walk humbly with your
God and fellowmen.

*"Pride goeth before destruction,
and an haughty spirit before a fall."*

– Proverbs 16:18

It was pride
that
cost

Chester
his
feathers.

Chester lived among the
rolling hills of Wisconsin,
in a winding valley where
breezes whisper through wild pink
roses and meadowlarks sing all day,
on a little farm called Pleasant Valley Farm.

Farmer Don
and Missus Dora
lived in the little
white house that sat
between two tall
oak trees.

In the big red hip-roofed barn
lived Dolly the milk cow, Danny the
workhorse, Shadow the barn cat,

and many other animals. But the
one I want to tell you about today is . . .

. . . Chester.

Chester was a buff Cochin rooster—
the only buff Cochin on the
whole farm.

Chester's
feathers were a
handsome golden yellow
that covered him from head to toe.

Other chickens lived on the farm—
black Australorps, brown banties, and
Rhode Island reds. But Chester was
the only yellow chicken on the place.
He was proud of that.

None of the
other chickens on the farm had feathers
all the way down their legs and toes, and none
was quite as big and grand as Chester. His tail was full and long,
gracefully flowing like liquid gold in a sweeping arch from his back.
Chester had some very fine feathers, and he was proud of them.

Every morning Chester stood on Danny's stall, puffed out his golden chest, and sang as the sun streaked the eastern sky with vibrant oranges, reds, purples, and pinks.

At the sound of his voice, Dolly the milk cow slowly rose from her bed of dewy grass in the pasture beyond the barn. One by one the other cows followed her example, and soon Dolly led the herd to the barn for the morning milking.

Chester had a strong voice, and he was proud of it.

Chester had a pretty black hen that went wherever he went, clucking and pecking contentedly beside him. She was a round, plump little hen who never failed to lay a fresh, warm brown egg in Danny's oat box each day. Chester was proud of his little black hen.

For such a big proud rooster,
Chester was a friendly fellow. And
curious. He loved to talk to the milkman, or
the feed salesman, or anyone who stopped by to
visit. If there was any excitement going on around the
farm, you would be sure to find Chester in the middle of it.

When the vet came to stitch up poor Buttercup's torn udder, Chester was right there, talking and clucking. He flew up onto the back of Doctor Miller's truck to watch and comment as the vet gathered his supplies. He escorted the doctor and Farmer Don to the stall where Buttercup was tied, and perched expectantly on a straw bale. But not for long. The view wasn't good enough from there.

As the vet bent over beneath Buttercup and began to work, Chester nudged his way under too.

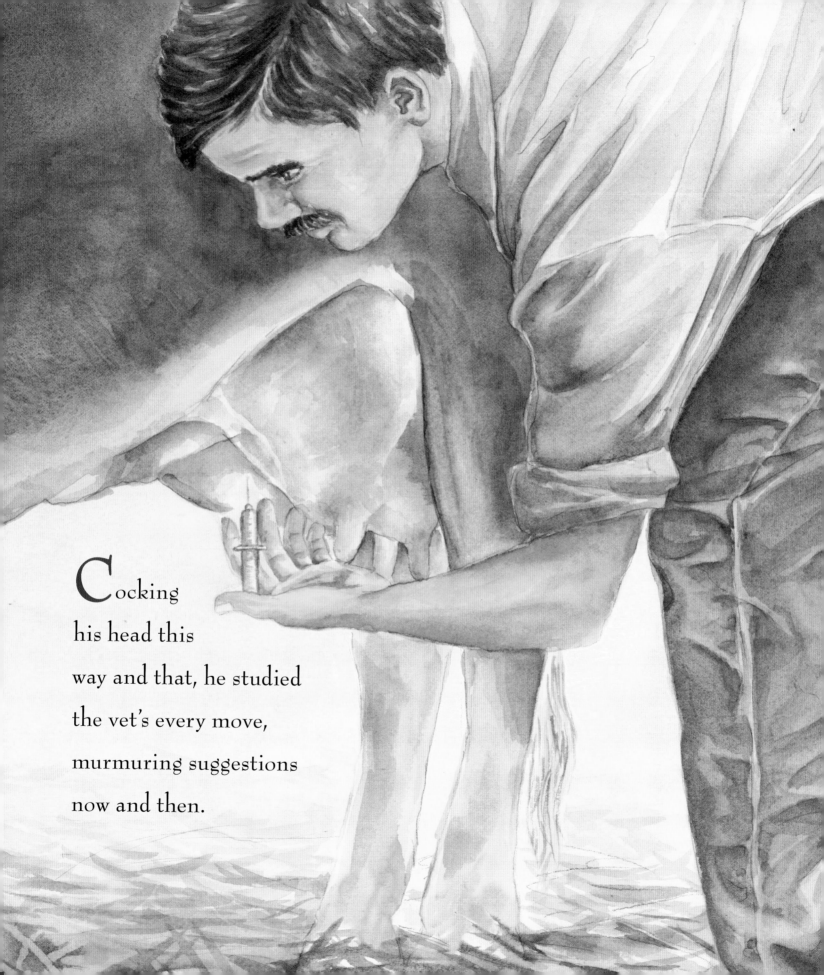

Cocking his head this way and that, he studied the vet's every move, murmuring suggestions now and then.

When Farmer
Don needed to fix the chain on the
manure spreader, Chester was right beside
him, clucking over the wrenches that Farmer Don
used, and advising that Farmer Don use the hammer next.

When Missus Dora pulled weeds in the garden, Chester was sure to be there. He never pulled any weeds, of course, but he clucked and crowed down the rows of peas and beans as Missus Dora worked.

Often he got in the way, because he had to inspect
every weed she pulled and examine each plant as
she weeded around it. Chester's little black hen
happily pecked at the long pink earthworms
that Missus Dora's weeding turned up.

Yes, Chester was big and handsome and friendly. But he was one proud rooster, and it was his pride that got him into trouble.

Chester thought he was the biggest, toughest, most handsome creature that ever walked on two legs. He had challenged all the other roosters on the farm and won. He had challenged the ducks and won. He had challenged the geese and won. He should have stopped there.

But Chester thought he was grand enough and tough enough to challenge Molly. And that was a mistake.

Molly was a large gray rabbit who lived under the corncrib. One of Molly's ears hung down while the other stood up. The ear that hung down had a large piece missing.

Molly had lived to a good old age by being sly and mean. She minded her own business as long as others minded theirs. But woe to any creature who invaded her territory or tried to dig their way into Molly's burrow beneath the weathered corncrib.

The cats had long since
learned to leave the mice
under the corncrib where they
were. They never crossed from
the barn to the machine shed
without looking twice for Molly.

The dogs had received some painful lessons before they learned to leave Molly alone. They were careful not to go too close to the corncrib. Even King, the white sheep dog, respected that battle-scarred rabbit.

Chester was fond of the fat yellow kernels
of corn that fell from the crib and lay
scattered on the ground.

Usually he waited
until Farmer Don
scooped the corn up in a
shovel and tossed it into the
barnyard for all the chickens
and ducks to share.

But this morning Chester didn't want to wait for Farmer Don. He would simply strut over to the corncrib and snatch the choicest kernels. If old Molly didn't like it,

she would have to face the biggest, toughest rooster on Pleasant Valley Farm.

This was one time Chester's little black hen would not follow him. She had no golden yellow feathers, and she was not as big as Chester, but she was wiser.

She was content to scratch and peck in the corn that Farmer Don tossed into the sunny barnyard.

So Chester approached the corncrib alone, warily cocking his fine golden head first one way, and then the other, watching for that rabbit.

There was no sign of Molly.

Chester became confident and crowed a challenge,
loud and clear. He flapped his golden wings
in the morning sunlight and helped
himself to several fat
kernels of corn.

There was
no sign
of Molly.

Chester moved closer to the corncrib.
He flapped and crowed.
He strutted and pecked.

Still there was
no sign of
Molly.

Chester decided that Molly must be afraid to face such a big tough rooster as he.

He strutted proudly up to the corncrib and crowed triumphantly. Then, cackling all the while, he peered beneath the door.

That's when there was a sign of Molly.

While Chester had been boasting and bragging with his fine, foolish head beneath the corncrib,

Molly had appeared from the other side.

In a gray streak
of fury, she pounced
on Chester's fine
feathered back.
With her
powerful
hind legs,
she ripped
out three
large patches
of golden
feathers.

Three hard
thumps,
and she was
gone.

Golden

yellow

feathers

floated

to the ground

as the dust settled.

Poor Chester!

No longer did his tail flow up and over in a sweeping golden arch.
All of his longest tail feathers were gone.
Most of the feathers
on his back were
missing too.

Chester looked sorry indeed.
He was not a handsome
yellow rooster now.

It took a whole year for Chester to grow back his fine feathers. Once again he was the grandest yellow rooster on Pleasant Valley Farm.

But even after his tail feathers had grown out
long and beautiful, Chester remembered
he was not so big and tough as he had thought.

He never challenged Molly again.

Helga Moser's *Pleasant Valley Farm Series*

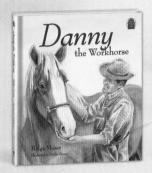
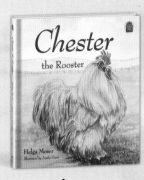
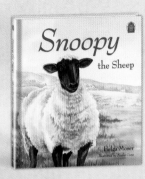

Danny
the Workhorse

Chester
the Rooster

Snoopy
the Sheep

Shadow
the Barn Cat

Christian Light Publications is a nonprofit, conservative Mennonite publishing company providing Christ-centered, Biblical literature including books, Gospel tracts, Sunday school materials, summer Bible school materials, and a full curriculum for Christian day schools and homeschools. Though produced primarily in English, some books, tracts, and school materials are also available in Spanish.

For more information about the ministry of CLP or its publications, or for spiritual help, please contact us at:

CHRISTIAN LIGHT PUBLICATIONS
P. O. Box 1212
Harrisonburg, VA 22803-1212

Telephone: 540-434-0768
Fax: 540-433-8896
E-mail: info@clp.org
Website: www.clp.org